SADDLEBACK *Classics*

ROBINSON CRUSOE

DANIEL DEFOE

ADAPTED BY

Stephen Feinstein

SADDLEBACK PUBLISHING, INC.

SADDLEBACK *Classics*

The Adventures of Tom Sawyer

Dr. Jekyll and Mr. Hyde

Dracula

Great Expectations

Jane Eyre

Moby Dick

Robinson Crusoe

The Time Machine

Development and Production: Laurel Associates, Inc.
Cover and Interior Art: Black Eagle Productions

SADDLEBACK PUBLISHING, INC.
3505 Cadillac Ave., Building F-9
Costa Mesa, CA 92626-1443

ISBN 1-56254-272-9

Printed in the United States of America
05 04 03   9 8 7 6 5 4 3 2 1

CONTENTS

The Call of the Sea

I was born in the year 1632, in the city of York in northern England. My father was a wealthy merchant from Germany who had moved to England. His name was Kreutznaer. But because this name was too difficult to say in English, he changed it to Crusoe. After settling in York, he married my mother, the daughter of a very good family. When I was born, I was named Robinson, my mother's family name.

I had two older brothers and two sisters. One brother was an officer in the British Army. He was killed in a battle near Dunkirk in England's war against the Spanish. I never knew my other brother. Nobody in the family seemed to know what had become of him. My father had always wanted me to become a lawyer. So he sent me to the finest schools. But I had my own ideas about how I wanted to live my life.

Ever since I was a young boy, I had been drawn to the sea. I used to enjoy sitting at the edge of the dock. There I would watch the tall sailing ships set out to sea. I would always wish that I could be going with them. I'd imagine that I was standing on board, waving to the people on the dock.

One day, when I was 18 years old, I dared to tell my parents about my longing for a life at sea. My father was very upset to hear this surprising news.

"You would be making a big mistake," he said. He had a sad look in his eyes. "Think about all that you would be giving up. Here you can have whatever your heart desires. You don't even have to work, if you would rather not. You have a family that loves you and a nice place to live. Who will look out for you at sea? You will be lonely so far from home. And life at sea is hard and dangerous. Think about what I am saying, son. Life at sea is not for you!"

I listened politely to my father's words. Then I said to him, "Perhaps you are right, Father. I will try not to think any more about the sea." But I knew that going to sea was what my heart still desired most of all.

About a year later, I was visiting Hull. Since this city was a major seaport, I went down to the docks. As I walked along the waterfront, I ran into an old friend of mine. He told me he was sailing that day on his father's ship to London.

"Why don't you come with me?" asked my friend. "Do come! It will be great fun."

My heart beat faster at his words. Here was my chance to go to sea. I could think of nothing else. In an instant I decided to go with my friend. As we climbed aboard the ship, my heart was filled with a wild joy.

It was the first of September, 1651. I was on board a ship bound for London. Now I felt that my life was truly beginning. Since this was my first time at sea, I had no idea of what to expect. Otherwise I might have begun to worry that the sky was growing black and the wind was kicking up.

No sooner did the ship sail out of the harbor and into the open sea than the wind began to howl. I stood on the deck as the sea began to rise. At first I enjoyed watching the waves and feeling the cold salty spray on my face. Soon, though, I began to feel sick because of the ship's rocking motion. As the ship tossed wildly about, I felt afraid for the first time. *Maybe my father was right. I should have stayed at home.*

The storm lasted for two days. I was seasick the whole time. But on the third day out, I walked up on deck. The sun shone in a clear blue sky. The sea was calm, its waves dancing in the sunlight. This was the most beautiful sight I had ever seen! Once again I heard the sea calling me.

A few days later the winds began to blow again. Soon another storm was upon us, worse than the last one. This time even the other sailors looked afraid. Huge waves washed over us. Then the mast snapped and

crashed to the deck. Soon the hull sprang several leaks and water came in faster than we could dump it out! The ship was clearly in danger of sinking.

The captain ordered all hands on deck. He fired a gun in the air to get the attention of another ship sailing close by. The sailors from the other ship helped get us off our ship and onto theirs. And not a moment too soon! Within 15 minutes our ship had sunk—without a trace of it remaining!

We were taken ashore at Yarmouth. Kind people in the town gave us places to spend the night. They also gave us enough money to travel on to London or back to Hull. The next day, while walking in town, I ran into my friend and his father, the captain.

"Young man," said the captain, "my son has told me all about you. Is it true that you sailed with us against your father's wishes?" I said yes, and then explained that this was to have been only the first leg of the voyages I planned.

The captain grew angry. "Let this be a warning to you! Now you know what horrors can happen at sea! Maybe you brought us bad luck, and that's why I lost my ship. Now, young man, don't be a fool! Go back to your father! Listen to his wise advice. You were not meant to be a sailor. Do not go to sea again, or you will meet with nothing but disaster!"

In truth, I was torn about which way to go. I knew the wise thing would have been to return home. That would have kept me safe and made my parents happy. As it was, a good bit of time had gone by until my poor, worried father learned that I had not gone down with the ship.

But something kept me from going home. What I still wanted, most of all, was to go to sea—to see the world and to seek my fortune. Since I had some money in my pocket—and being young and foolish—I decided to travel on to London.

2 Shipwrecked

When I arrived in London, I had second thoughts about what I was doing. A voice inside me was telling me to go back home. But I also kept hearing the sea calling to me. And there was something else: I was afraid that if I returned home, my family and the neighbors would laugh at me. Just thinking about them made me feel ashamed.

By chance, I met the captain of a trading ship that was going to Guinea, on the west coast of Africa. We soon became friends, and he invited me to sail with him to Africa. On his advice, I borrowed some money, about 40 pounds, from my relatives. I then bought various goods to trade in Africa.

On the voyage to Guinea, I learned everything I needed to know about sailing a ship. The helpful captain also taught me how to be a merchant. Before returning to England, I had turned my 40 pounds into 300 pounds! I was very happy, and could hardly wait till my next adventure.

Sadly, shortly after our return to England, my friend the captain died. I decided to sail again to Guinea. This time the ship was under the command of the man who had been the captain's mate. Had I known how this voyage would turn out, I never would have left my homeland.

One gray morning, our ship was sailing south, midway between the Canary Islands and the coast of Africa. Suddenly we noticed another ship heading in our direction. As it got closer, the captain shouted, *"Pirates!"*

We tried to outrun the pirates, but their ship steadily gained on us. We knew they would be upon us in a few hours, so we prepared to fight. Our ship had 12 guns, but the pirates had 18. About 3:00 in the afternoon they caught up with us. A fierce battle followed. Our ship was destroyed and some of our men were killed. The rest of the crew were taken prisoner by the pirates, whom we discovered to be Moors.

The pirates took us to a place called Sallee, a port on the northern coast of Africa. The pirate captain took me home with him. Because I was young and strong, he had decided to keep me as his slave! At first, I was somewhat glad about this. I hoped that my master would take me out to sea with him. If I was lucky, his ship would be captured by an English or Spanish warship. Then I would be set free.

But sadly, this was not to be. Whenever my master went to sea, he left me on shore to do housework and look after his little garden. Then, when he returned home, I had to go onto the ship and clean it up.

Whenever I remembered my father's words, I was filled with regret. All I ever thought about was a plan of escape. But escape was not possible. My master's men kept constant watch over me.

Two years later, I was still a prisoner.

Over time, my master had begun to trust me. Every so often he would send me out in the harbor on a small boat to catch fish for his dinner. One of the Moors had always come with me. One day, however, my master asked for fish. Because none of the Moors were around, he allowed me to go fishing by myself.

I could hardly believe my good luck! I rowed the little boat out into the harbor. There was no wind at all that day. A thick fog hung over the water's surface. After rowing a half mile, I could no longer see the shore. Since there wasn't a breeze, the boat's small sail was useless. So I just kept rowing until I was far beyond the harbor and heading out to sea.

That night the wind picked up. For two days I sailed along the African coast. Finally, a passing ship spotted me and picked me up. The captain of the ship was from Portugal. He told me that his ship was on its way to Brazil.

I was so happy to be rescued that I told

the captain he could keep the little sailboat. He refused to accept any payment for saving me. "I have saved your life," he said, "as I would have expected you to save mine."

When we arrived in Brazil, the kind captain gave me some money for the little boat. Then he introduced me to some friends of his who owned sugar plantations. I decided to buy some property. The planters helped me get started farming the land.

Several years later, I was the owner of a fine sugar plantation. But I really did not enjoy farming. Often I would find myself daydreaming about the sea.

My planter friends could see that I was becoming unhappy and restless. Then one day, they said they had an interesting idea that might appeal to me. Over the years I had spoken to them about my trading adventures in Guinea. Now they had decided to send a ship to Africa in order to do some trading. They believed this would make them very rich men. And they were hoping that I might be willing to sail the ship for them.

This was music to my ears! I got excited about the idea of going to sea again. My friends also said that they would pay for the whole trip. It wouldn't cost me a penny.

Of course, I had little experience. I had not the faintest clue about what this trip would end up costing me. So, I gladly accepted their offer.

On September 1, 1659—exactly eight years after I had first set foot on my friend's ship in Hull—I set sail for Africa. For the first 12 days at sea, although the weather was quite hot, I was in heaven! I had forgotten the wonderful smell of salt air, and how beautiful the sea can be. I loved listening to the wind in the rigging, and the cries of the seagulls. I didn't even get seasick from the constant rising and falling motion of the ship.

Then my luck ran out! On the 12th day, we were caught in a terrible storm. In the darkness, I could see waves towering around the ship like mountains. For the next 12 days the storm raged. Indeed, the storm was so violent it must have been a hurricane. We were blown off course so far that we had no idea of where we were!

Then, one morning, a sailor cried out, "*Land!*" The storm was still raging. We were afraid our ship would be smashed to pieces on the rocks near the shore. So I ordered the whole crew into the longboat. Terrified, we rowed toward shore like men going to their deaths. Then a huge wave washed over us. The boat flipped over, and we were tossed into the churning waters. In a moment, every man of us was swallowed up!

What happened next is still not very clear in my memory. Yet somehow I was able to keep myself from drowning. I was a good swimmer, but I was caught deep in the body of a wave. In fact I was ready to burst from holding my breath.

I could feel myself being carried toward the shore by a mighty force. Then my hands and head shot above the surface of the water, and I gasped for air. Next I felt the ground under my feet, and I tried to run out of the water. But another wave knocked me off my feet. I would have been dragged back out to sea if I hadn't held fast to a big rock. Before the next wave could catch me, I managed to crawl out of the water and onto the sandy beach.

For a few minutes I lay there, choking and gasping. Then I saw that water from the breaking waves was rushing toward me across the wet sand. So I got up and limped across the narrow beach. I climbed a little cliff and fell down upon the grass. There I was free from danger, quite out of the water's reach. With a heart full of gratitude, I looked up and thanked God for saving my life.

3 Settling In

After I had rested a while, I walked about on the beach. I couldn't believe how lucky I was to still be alive. Although I was soaking wet, I did not feel the cold because the air was so warm. The wind was still blowing, however, and the rain was falling in sheets.

Hoping to find the other sailors, I searched up and down the beach. But I could find no sign of them or the longboat. Could it be that I was the only one still alive? Then I came across something that made my heart sink. There, at the edge of the water, were three sailor's hats and two shoes. This was all that remained of my crew!

Soon after this sad discovery, I learned something that made me feel even worse.

The storm had let up by now. The strong winds had died down, and the heavy rain had turned to sprinkles. I was now able to see a long way out over the ocean. There, far out beyond the rocks, was our ship! It was still afloat, still in one piece. Had we only stayed on board, all of us would still be alive!

I sat down on the beach, deep in thought. What was done was done. Nothing could bring back those men. Now I had to face the fact that I was alone. I had no idea where I was. Most likely I was on an island, but I did not know which one. Perhaps there were other people living here. If they were friendly, they might be willing to help me. If they were not friendly—well, I might be in real trouble. It could also be that I was the *only* living person on this dot of land.

The longer I thought about it, the more frightened I felt. After all, how was I going to live? I had nothing to eat or drink. So how was I going to keep from starving or dying of thirst? I had no weapon, not even a knife.

So I couldn't hunt animals, if there were any around. And if there were wild beasts on the island, they could easily attack me and kill me.

I began to panic. For a while, I jumped up and ran about like a madman. When I calmed down, it was getting dark. Where should I spend the night? I asked myself. Where would I be safe? I knew it was the habit of wild beasts to hunt at night.

I turned away from the beach and climbed back up the cliff. Near me was a thick, bushy tree somewhat like a fir, but thorny. I decided to spend the night in the treetop. At least wild beasts would not be able to get to me there.

But first, I went looking for fresh water to drink. I was very thirsty. To my great joy, I found a spring. Then, having drunk the water, I climbed the tree. I placed myself carefully among the branches.

Now I was too tired to think any longer. As yet I could see no way that I could go on living here. "Tomorrow I'll choose which way I am going to die," I said to myself. Then I fell fast asleep.

When I awoke the next day, the sun was already high in the sky. It was a beautiful day. As I gazed out at the sea, I saw that the ship had drifted to within a mile of the shore. Even at this distance, I could see that the ship had been damaged beyond repair. Then I thought about all of the supplies that were stowed on board. "Maybe I can save some of those things," I said to myself.

The sea was calm and the tide was low. It was an easy swim out to the ship. At first, I didn't know how I could climb aboard, so I swam around to the other side of the ship. There I saw a rope hanging down from the deck, and I climbed up.

By some kind of miracle, the part of the ship where the food was stored had kept dry. As soon as I found the bread, I ate half a loaf. There was also some rice, three Dutch cheeses, and five pieces of dried goat meat.

Then I looked for the kinds of things that would be most useful on shore. I found the carpenter's chest—a most useful prize—which was full of tools I would need on shore. I also found some guns, gunpowder, powder horns, a small bag of shot, and two rusty old swords. I gathered these things together with my supply of food.

Now I had to figure out a way to carry these supplies ashore. If I could build a raft, that would solve the problem. I looked around the ship. All I needed was some wood. Gazing up at the masts, an idea suddenly came to me. Since this ship was never going to sail anywhere again, it did not need its masts.

There was a saw in the carpenter's chest. I quickly went to work. After sawing up the masts, I tied them together with rope. In less than two hours, I had my raft! I lowered the raft over the side of the ship and loaded my supplies. Then I climbed down onto it. Fortunately, the tide was just coming in. It soon carried the raft back toward shore. I rowed the raft into a narrow inlet. Then I unloaded the goods on a stretch of dry, sandy beach along the shore.

I looked for a place to build a camp of sorts. I wanted my place to be safe from attack—from wild animals *or* from people. I found my spot partway up a hill that was just beyond the inlet. Right behind my spot was a very large rock. From this rise of the hill, I could keep watch for any ships at sea.

During the next two weeks I made ten more trips to the ship. Each time I rowed the raft out to the ship during low tide. I brought back sails, nails, barrels of flour, a box of sugar, corn, ropes, chains, some books, and such clothes as I would need. I also brought back a dog and two cats.

I even brought back some money I had found in the ship's safe. At first, the idea of keeping the money made me laugh. Just then, money seemed to me the most useless thing in the world—like a creature not worth rescuing. But I kept it anyway.

Up on my hill, I used the sails and some boards I had saved from the ship to build a tent. Little by little, I carried all of my things up the hill and stored them in my tent.

It was good that I had gotten all of the supplies off the ship when I did. Soon the pleasant weather changed. The wind began blowing. I knew that before long another storm would be raging. I was right. The next day I watched sadly as the ship was torn apart and the pieces swept out to sea.

Alone on an Island

When the storm was over, I stepped outside of my tent. Once again, the weather was fine. There was not even a single cloud in the blue sky. I climbed all the way to the top of my hill and looked in every direction.

Now I knew for sure that I was on an island. I could see some rocks and two smaller islands to the west. But in every other direction was nothing but the sea. And I could see no signs of other people on the island. There were no houses, roads, or even trails. So I now knew that I was all alone.

Whether I lived or died would be completely up to me. I would soon find out if I was clever enough to survive by myself. When I got back to my camp, I picked up one of the guns and went looking for game.

As I came to the edge of a wooded area, I saw a large bird sitting on a tree. I aimed my gun and fired. There was a sudden explosion of wild screeches as a great many different kinds of birds flew up out of the trees. None of the birds looked familiar to me, but the one I had aimed at fell to the ground. Now I saw that it looked like some type of hawk. Unfortunately, its flesh was not fit to eat.

Later I walked into the woods, hoping to find food that would be more suitable, perhaps some sort of fowl. Before long, I found the type of bird I was looking for. I shot two fowls that were something like ducks. I brought them back to my camp, and found them very good to eat.

Protecting myself from dangerous beasts or men was one of my main concerns. I decided to set up my camp quickly so that I would be as safe as possible. As much as I could, I wanted to turn my camp into a fortress. After giving it some thought, I came up with a plan.

There was a wide crack in the rock wall behind my tent. I thought that I might be able to dig into the crack and create a storage space. By removing a good deal of earth and rocks from the crack, I made myself a cave. This turned out to be a safe, dry place to keep my things. In fact it served as my cellar. It also was a good place to build a fire during rainy weather.

The other part of my plan was to build a wooden fence. I began by drawing a half circle around my camp. In this half circle I placed two rows of strong stakes. I drove them into the ground until they stood very firm. The stakes were sharpened on the top, and about five and a half feet tall. I carefully placed the two long rows of stakes about six inches apart.

It took me a long time, almost a year, to complete the fence. Cutting the stakes in the woods, bringing them to my camp, and driving them into the ground was hard work. The complete process took three days for each stake. I did not build a door in the fence as an entrance to my fortress. Instead, I used a short ladder to go over the top. Once inside, I lifted the ladder over the fence after me. Inside, I felt completely safe.

Each day, if it wasn't raining, I would spend a few hours exploring the island. I always took my gun along, hoping to find something to shoot for food. And I always took my dog with me. Often I would find and shoot the ducklike birds.

One day I came across some wild goats. They ran away from me before I could get close enough to shoot one. In the following days, I kept a careful watch for them. But they were very quick and shy. Whenever I came across them, they would run away in a terrible fright. Finally, one day, I managed to shoot one. I was happy to have fresh meat.

I was always thinking about ways to make my life better. Early on I had set up a hammock. This was much more comfortable than sleeping on the hard ground.

During the following weeks and months, I set about making various things I needed.

One day, for example, I decided I needed a table. In the past, I had never learned to use tools to build things. Nobody had ever taught me how to make a table. So I had to figure out how to do it myself.

After I had a table, I made some chairs. These were more difficult. My first few tries ended in failure, but I kept working at it. Finally I had chairs that I could use. Then I built shelves upon which to store my supplies. Next I made some wooden baskets so that I could hang up my food to keep it away from the dog and cats. I learned that with enough time to think and plan carefully, I could make whatever I needed.

After my first few days on the island, I became afraid that I would soon lose my reckoning of time. How could I separate the Sabbath days from the working days? How would I know how many weeks, months—or years—had passed? Except for changes in the weather, each day was more or less the same for me. So I came up with a plan. I set up a large wooden post. I cut a notch in

it with my knife for each day, starting with September 30, 1659. That was the day I first came ashore. I made a longer cut for every Sunday. This is how I kept my calendar.

Some days my lonely island life made my heart sore, and I would feel sorry for myself. Except for the dog and the cats, I had no company. I wished that I could teach them to talk. Often I did speak to them, and they sometimes seemed to understand me. But of course, there was never an answering word.

What manner of life had I been reduced to? Beyond my lonely fears, what was the true state of my affairs? I needed to make an accurate account of my situation. I decided to weigh the comforts I enjoyed against the miseries I suffered.

In order to help sort out my thoughts, I decided to write everything down. First I listed the things about my life that were bad. Then I tried to balance out these items with things that were good.

Bad: *I'm stuck on a horrible, lonely island, with no hope of ever being rescued.*

Good: *But I'm alive, and not drowned, as were all the others on the ship.*

Bad: *I've been singled out and separated from the rest of the world to be unhappy.*

Good: *But I've been singled out, too, from all the ship's crew to be spared from death. He that saved me from death can save me from this condition.*

Bad: *I don't have another person to speak to.*

Good: *God sent the ship near enough to*

shore that I could get all the things I need to live on this island as long as I must.

Now I was able to consider the *whole* of my condition. As I studied my list, I made a wonderful discovery: *There is something positive that we may be thankful for in any unhappy situation.*

So the days and weeks passed. The months passed. My life pretty much followed the same pattern from one day to the next. During the rainy weather I spent less time outdoors. During fair weather I spent more time exploring the island.

Happy Days

During my first summer on the island, I became ill with a fever. For many days I lay in my hammock, too weak to get up. First I would feel like I was burning up. This lasted for hours on end. Then I would shake with chills. Then I would feel hot again. For days I felt too sick to eat or drink. I became afraid that I would never get well.

As I lay sick in my hammock, I began to feel very sorry for myself. I remembered my father's words: *"You will be lonely so far from home."* And now here I was, sick and alone, with nobody at all to take care of me. These sad thoughts brought tears to my eyes.

But then I began to think deeply about the meaning of life. The big questions about life and death ran through my mind.

"What am I, and all the other creatures?" I wondered. "What is this earth and sea, of which I have seen so much? Who made the world?"

I had to remind myself that it was a miracle that I was still alive. After all, I alone had survived the shipwreck. I began to pray for the first time in my life. Soon I was able to stop feeling sorry for myself. Instead, I felt sorry for the sadness I had caused my father and my mother.

When the fever passed, my strength slowly returned. Before long, I was up and about. I was now feeling much better, and I was thankful for my good health. Soon, I began to explore the island again. Every day I went out walking with my gun and dog.

I began looking at things in a new way. The island now seemed to be a place of great beauty! I looked up at the trees swaying in the sea breeze. I breathed deeply of the salt air, and I listened to the sound of the surf. Why did a person have to live in a place such as England to be happy? I now thought that

I could be perfectly happy on my island.

Then I made another discovery that filled me with joy. On one of my walks, I came upon a valley I had never seen before. Growing here in the sun were bunches of ripe, purple grapes ready to be picked. I also found juicy melons and trees bearing oranges, lemons, and limes.

Then I came to a clearing in the woods. A sudden idea flashed in my mind. This spot would be a good place to live, at least part of the time. I decided that someday I would build a second home, a "country home," right in this clearing. But now I went back to pick the grapes I had found. Near my tent I hung the grapes up on the branches of a tree. There they would dry into raisins in the hot sun.

During the next few weeks, I set up a tent on the spot I had chosen for my country house. This would be a good place for a farm, I thought. Then I built a fence around the place. In a few days I harvested more than 200 bunches of raisins from the grapes

I had put out in the sun. I took them back to my fortress and stored them in my cave. The timing was perfect! No sooner had I finished storing the raisins than it began to rain. The rain continued for several days. I didn't mind, however. Knowing that I would have raisins to eat for the rest of the year made me very happy.

One day, I was looking through the things in my cave. By now, the cave had become more than just a storage space or cellar. It had become another part of my living space—my kitchen and dining room.

As I looked around, I found a little bag from the ship. I took it outside and studied it closely. It had once held grain but was now almost empty. Rats on the ship must have eaten the grain. Now I thought I could use the bag to hold my gunpowder. So I shook what was left of the grain out of the bag. A few seeds fell to the ground.

About a month later, I had a pleasant surprise. I found barley and rice growing where the seeds had dropped. The young

plants were beautiful. I harvested the grain when it was ripe and then planted the seeds again. I planned to continue doing so until I had enough grain to make bread.

In my cave I also found a bag of corn that had been partly eaten by rats on the ship. I threw the corn away. Later, I was very happy to see corn growing on that spot.

On September 30, I had been on the island for one year. I decided to make this a special day, a day of fasting and prayer.

I knew that I was lucky, and I truly felt glad to be alive. By now I was quite pleased with my life on the island. So I gave humble thanks to God for taking such good care of me!

During my first year on the island, there had been two dry seasons and two rainy seasons. I figured that if this was the usual weather pattern, I should be able to get two harvests a year. If I planted barley, rice, and corn in February, the spring rains in March and April would water them. Later in the year, I could plant again during the second dry season. Then the second rainy season would provide water.

I ended up with more barley, rice, and corn than I needed. So I stored most of my harvest in baskets inside the cave. During the rainy weather, I made more baskets for storage. I also set about making pots and jars. I did this by shaping earth into pots and putting them out in the sun to dry. As they dried, however, they cracked and broke. But I kept trying, and in two months I had a few strange looking earthen jars.

It was then I noticed a broken piece of a jar in the fire. It had turned hard as stone. *Of course!* Why hadn't I thought of it sooner! Now I took all of my earthen pots and put them over the fire. There they sat on the hot coals, heating up all night long. By morning, I had five good cooking pots.

At about this time, I ate the last of my bread from the ship. I thought about how to bake bread. I ground up some of my barley and rice into flour. I mixed the flour with water, seasonings, and fat from the game I had shot. Then I formed loaves. Now I needed an oven. I placed a slab of stone near the fire and laid my loaves on it. I covered the slab with a large earthen pot turned upside down. Then I raked live coals from the fire over the pot. In a while I brushed away the coals and removed the pot. I was delighted with the results—barley bread and rice cakes as good as any ever baked in the finest ovens of the world!

When the weather was good, I still explored other parts of the island. One day

I found turtles on the far side of the island. I collected a bunch of turtle eggs from the beach. Then, on the way home, my dog caught a young wild goat. I quickly stopped the dog from killing the goat, and brought the little animal home with me. Someday, I hoped to raise a herd of tame goats.

On another trip across the island, I caught a parrot. I brought the bird home with me and built a cage. Then I began teaching it to talk. Even though it was a wild creature, the parrot seemed happy to be with me. The first thing he said was "Poll." I thought he was telling me his name. So from then on I called him Poll. I was very happy to hear a voice other than my own.

My second year on the island was coming to an end. I thought that my life in this faraway place had made me a better and happier man. On September 30, I fasted and gave a special prayer of thanks to God for protecting me.

 **The Canoe**

During the next few years, life on the island was very peaceful. With each harvest I had more and more grain. I hunted nearly every day, and there was always plenty of fresh fruit. I no longer had any worries about not having enough to eat.

I built my "country house" in the valley I had discovered. I always made sure to spend part of each year there.

When my clothes finally began to wear out, I taught myself to make new ones. I used the dried skins of the animals I had killed for meat. By trial and error I made a hat, coat, and pants. I also made an umbrella to protect myself from the rain and the sun.

One day I climbed a tall hill on the other side of the island. The day was so clear that

I caught sight of land—way off in the distance! It was so far away that I could not tell whether it was another island or the coast of South America. I had once read that the people who lived near that coast were savages. Now I said to myself, "Thank God that I was shipwrecked on this island instead of over there!"

But the sight of another body of land made me think again about how alone I was on my island. I was no longer unhappy to be living on the island. But deep inside, I found that I still wished for escape.

I decided to build a canoe, one that was large enough to make an ocean voyage. I chose a large tree in the woods. Then I went to work with my axe. The trunk was so thick that it took me 20 days to cut the tree down. Then I worked for about a month carving the tree into the shape of a canoe. It took me another three months just to hollow out the inside.

Finally I had a canoe—a *huge* canoe—the biggest such vessel I had ever seen!

Surely this boat would be sturdy enough to cross the sea. Many a weary stroke it had cost, you may be sure. But who grudges pains when deliverance is in view?

Then all of a sudden, I saw that there was a big problem with the canoe. I had made a bad mistake. My canoe was sitting at the edge of the woods, not on the shore. It was so heavy that I couldn't move it an inch. How was I going to get it down to the ocean? Now I had to admit to myself that this canoe was not going anywhere! I had been very foolish. Next time I would have to plan better.

The next year, I decided to try again. I built a canoe out of a smaller tree trunk. Then I dug a narrow canal from the woods to the shore. This work took me about two years.

Finally, on November 6, during my sixth year on the island, I was ready to sail. I loaded the canoe with supplies—barley, bread, rice, meat, fruit, and gunpowder. With a great deal of effort, I was able to push the small craft into the canal. Then I climbed in and floated the canoe out to the sea.

I had already built a mast and a sail for my canoe, and now I set up my umbrella at the back. I sat under its shade and looked out at the sea. It felt good to be on a boat again. My plan was to sail around the island. I wanted to try out the canoe on a short trip before setting out on an ocean voyage.

It was a fine day, and the sea seemed to be calm. But a strong current was pulling me out toward the open sea. Suddenly, I saw that I was in danger! The current was carrying the canoe toward some rocks that stuck up out of the water. I was afraid it would crash against the rocks! I grabbed the sides of the canoe and held my breath. But at the last minute, the current swept the canoe safely around the rocks and carried me farther out to sea.

I thought to myself, "Why did I want to leave my beautiful island? I was happy there. I should have stayed where I was."

As my little canoe bounced around on the waves, I looked back at my island. It was now far off in the distance, becoming so small I could hardly see it. I looked around me at the wide open sea. A huge wave splashed over the side of the canoe, dousing me from head to toe! Suddenly an ocean voyage in the little canoe didn't seem like such a good idea. In fact, I didn't even want to sail all the way around the island. What I really wanted was to return, safe and sound, to my fortress on the island.

Then a gentle wind began to blow. It seemed that luck was with me that day. I jumped up and set the sail. As the wind caught the sail, it pushed the canoe back toward the island. But as I got closer, the wind suddenly died down. Then another current caught the canoe and carried it around to the other side of the island.

Finally I was able to guide my canoe into the mouth of a little stream. At last I could leap into the water and push the canoe onto the shore. I dropped down on the sand and thanked God that I was safe!

I quickly found a good hiding place for the canoe under some bushes. It came to me that I probably would never use the canoe again. I gave up all thoughts of escape from the island. But my canoe would be safe in its hiding place in case I ever changed my mind.

Carrying my umbrella over my head, I walked across the island toward my fortress. I was feeling very tired. When I reached my home, I went inside to rest. Drained of all energy, I fell asleep right away.

A voice woke me from a dream. It was saying, "Robin, Robinson Crusoe! Where have you been? Poor Robin!" I knew that voice—it sounded like my own voice! I looked up. It was Poll, my parrot! Poll sounded sad. He must have missed me. I was happy for this welcome, and indeed I felt very content to be back.

I was through with sea voyages. During the next few years I was happy again on my island. I finally decided it was time to raise a herd of goats, so I built a trap. In a few days I caught several wild goats, both large older ones and little young ones.

I let the older goats go, and tied the little

ones inside a pen. I had built the pen—a simple fence around an open field—near my country home. There was fresh water and grass for grazing inside the pen. The little goats lived happily there and grew up to be tame. In three years, I had my own dairy—more than 40 goats in five different pastures. From my herd of goats I got plenty of milk to make cheese and butter.

By now I had been on the island for 15 years. I felt that I was a very lucky man.

Whenever I stayed at my fortress, I served dinner each night at the table in the cave. There was always plenty of good food to eat. And for company, I still had my dog, two cats, and Poll.

Then one day I was walking along the shore on the far side of the island. As usual, I was carrying my gun. Then something on the ground caught my eye. I bent down for a closer look, and an icy chill suddenly went down my spine. There in the sand was a footprint—a *man*'s footprint!

7 Cannibals

I bent down to examine the footprint. Perhaps I was mistaken. Surely it could not really be a human footprint! But, no, this was a clear print of a foot. There were toes, a heel, and every part of a human foot. I looked all around to see if there were anymore prints, but I could find none. How this one footprint got here, I could not in the least imagine.

It was clear that whoever made the footprint had not worn shoes. Perhaps it had been made by a savage! Now it came to me that I could be in great danger!

I held myself perfectly still. I was almost afraid to breathe. Perhaps the savage was watching me from the woods above the shore. I was afraid to turn around. I listened carefully for sounds of another person. But all I could hear was the sound of the waves breaking on the shore.

My heart was beating fast, and I was still too afraid to move. It seemed as if I sat there for an hour, but I'm sure it was only a few minutes. Finally, I stood up and began running down the beach. My feet flew. I dashed through the woods and over the hills to my own side of the island.

For all I knew, the savage could be following me. Every few steps I looked behind me. A few times I thought I saw someone, but it was always just a bush or a tree. I was gasping for breath. But I kept running until I was safe inside my fortress. That night I could not sleep at all.

For the next few days I didn't dare leave my fortress. I got very little sleep, because I could not stop worrying. I had lived on the island for more than 15 years. In all that time, I had seen no signs of another human being. So I knew that savages did not live anywhere on my island. But now, perhaps they had found out that *I* lived here. They might have found something that belonged to me. Or, even worse, they might have seen me!

The footprint had put a sudden end to all the peace and happiness I had found on the island. Now I couldn't stop thinking that the savages might be coming to kill me! I no longer felt safe, even inside my fortress. Fear is a terrible thing. When terror takes over your mind, it's hard to think straight.

After five days had passed, I forced myself to leave my fortress. I went back to the other side of the island to have another look at the footprint. "What if the strange footprint was my own?" I wondered. Maybe there was really nothing—or no one—for me to fear.

When I found the footprint again, I studied it carefully. Then I placed my own foot next to it. They did not match. The footprint was clearly bigger than my own foot. Also, I could not remember ever having walked barefoot on this beach.

I returned to my fortress. "There must be something I can do to make this place safer,"

I said to myself. After thinking long and hard, I came up with a plan. I would build a second fence or wall outside my first fence.

It took me many months to build the second wall. I used slices of tree branches, old cables, and anything else I could think of to make the wall thick. Then I cut tiny openings in the wall, and I positioned a gun inside each. Placed this way in the wall, the guns were like cannons. Finally, when the wall was completed, I began to relax and feel a little safer.

Along the ground in front of the wall I planted a row of trees. In a few years, I was sure, my fortress would be well hidden behind a grove of thick greenery.

During the next three years, I left my fortress only to take care of my goats and my country house. I hardly ever went anywhere else on the island. In truth, I could never forget the day I had discovered the strange footprint. I wondered if the savages had come back to visit my island since that time. So one day I walked back to the sandy shore on the other side of the island.

What I found on the beach made my skin crawl. I came across the remains of a fire in a pit in the sand. Scattered all around the fire pit were bones—*human* bones! I looked in horror at several skulls, ribs, arm bones, and leg bones. It didn't take long to figure out what had happened here. There had been a feast. The savages who were taking part in the feast had to be cannibals—eaters of human flesh!

This thought made me sick to my stomach. On the way back to my fortress, I thought about different ways that I could get rid of the cannibals. It seemed that they only visited the other side of the island, so I was probably safe on my own side. Perhaps I could watch for their return from a hiding place in the woods. Then, when they came ashore, I could kill them with my guns.

I found a good hiding place in the woods above the shore on the other side of the island. Nobody could see me there, and I had a clear view of the beach. For more than two months, I spent most of my days there. All I could think was that savages such as these must certainly be evil. They didn't deserve to live. But in time, another thought came to me. Wasn't it possible that, according to their own beliefs, there was nothing wrong with eating human flesh? After all, Englishmen saw nothing wrong with eating beef, or pork, or lamb.

I decided that I no longer had any right to kill the cannibals. But I would still watch for them and for any sign that they were preparing another feast. Perhaps I could save someone from becoming a meal for them. So for several more months, I spent a lot of time in my hiding place, keeping watch for visiting cannibals.

But the cannibals didn't return. Finally I began to worry less and less about them. And when I stopped watching for them, my life returned to normal.

One day, after I had been on the island for 22 years, the fear returned. I woke up very early that morning, before the sun was up. I was walking up the hill behind my fortress when something odd caught my eye. I thought I saw a flicker of light on the beach far up the coast. How strange! Whatever could it be? I ran down to my cave and got my telescope. Then I climbed up to the top of the hill to get a better view.

When I looked through my telescope, I could see that the flicker of light was a fire on the beach. People were dancing around the fire. "Oh, merciful God!" I thought. "It's the cannibals—and this time they're on *my* side of the island!" They were only about two miles away. As I watched, the tide came in. Then the savages stopped dancing and rowed off in their boats.

I went inside my cave, grabbed my gun, and quickly ran down to the beach. As I walked along the shore toward the fire, the sun came up. By the time I got there, the fire was out. But what I saw around the fire pit filled me with horror. Once again, I saw the signs of a cannibal feast—human bones. Once again, I felt sure that my life was in terrible danger. I had a dreadful feeling that someday I would come face to face with the cannibals. It was just a matter of time.

§8 Friday

One night I slept restlessly. In a strange dream, I saw the cannibals rowing back to my island. By this time I had been on the island for 24 years. During the past two years I had not seen any sign of cannibals— or any other visitors. But since I had a dream about them, they must have still been in the back of my mind.

In my fretful dream, the cannibals began to prepare a feast. They held a prisoner, and were getting ready to kill and then eat the poor man. But for a few minutes they did not pay attention to their prisoner. Suddenly, the man sprang to his feet and ran away. Making his escape from the cannibals, he kept on running until he got to my fortress. I gave him a warm greeting, and took him in.

I was very happy to have company. After all, I had not spoken to another human being in 24 years! Then I woke up. "Oh, no! It was only a dream," I said sadly. The joy that I had felt was gone in an instant. Then I knew that I would never again be truly happy until I had another person for company.

Another year went by with no sign of the cannibals. Then, one day in 1684, I was looking out to sea through my telescope. To my great surprise, five canoes were heading toward the shore on *my* side of the island. It was the cannibals! They came ashore about two miles away from me. It was the same place where they had made the fire on their last visit.

As I watched them, I counted close to 30 men. They were dragging two prisoners with them. Suddenly they knocked one of their prisoners down with a club. They continued to beat the man while he was down. Finally they stopped. The man wasn't moving— perhaps he was dead. While the cannibals were busy with this prisoner, the other one broke away. He ran along the beach in the direction of my fortress. Then the cannibals saw that he was trying to escape. Two of them chased after him.

Suddenly I remembered my dream about the cannibals. It seemed that it was coming true! I grabbed a gun and took off running toward the prisoner. I knew I had to do whatever I could to save the man. When I got close to him, two of the cannibals had almost caught up with him. I pointed my gun and fired. One cannibal went down. Then I fired again and got the other one.

Meanwhile, the prisoner looked at me with eyes full of fear. The sound of my gunfire had scared him. He looked as if he was about to take off running again. But somehow, with hand signals, I was able to make him understand that I meant him no harm. When I smiled at him, he spoke in a language I had never heard before. Although I did not understand one word, it was wonderful to hear a human voice. It was the sweetest sound I had heard in 25 years!

The man came up to me, knelt down, and kissed the ground. Then he laid his head upon the ground. Taking hold of my foot, he set my foot upon his head. I believe that this was his way of thanking me for saving his life. Next he quickly dug a hole in the sand and buried the two dead cannibals. I saw that he was an intelligent man, although he looked like a savage. Now the other cannibals would not find them if they should come after us.

I began speaking to the man I had saved. I wanted to begin teaching him English right away. I felt that my prayer had finally been answered. At last I would have someone to speak to.

I decided to call the man Friday because that was the day I saved his life. I pointed to him and said, "Friday, Fri-day!" He seemed to catch on right away. Soon he pointed to himself and repeated after me, "Fri-day!" Then I pointed to myself and taught him to say "Master."

I brought Friday back to my fortress. To

show him welcome, I gave him milk in an earthen pot and some bread. I let him see me drink it and dip my bread in it. I said "Friday, eat!" He ate the food, carefully copying what I did. He looked around with interest at all of my things. I soon came to understand that he wanted to serve me because I had saved his life. He wanted to help me in any way he could.

I was glad that the rest of the cannibals had not been able to find us. Later that afternoon, Friday and I climbed the hill behind the fortress. Through my telescope, as the tide came in, I saw the cannibals leave the island in their canoes.

Although I was very happy to have Friday stay at my place, I was not used to sharing anything with another person. Friday seemed very happy to be there. But how did I know if I could trust him? After all, the man was a total stranger. That night I set up a bed for Friday between my two fences. I slept in my cave, and I barred the door. But I found that I didn't need to be so careful. I soon learned that I could trust Friday with my life.

The next day, I gave my new companion a pair of pants to wear. I then made other items of clothing for him from animal skins. In the days ahead, I taught Friday how to make bread. I showed him how to grind the rice and barley into flour and how to bake it. He seemed eager to please me, and he learned quickly. Then I showed him how to plant corn, and how to pick grapes and dry them into raisins. I even showed him how to take care of the goats.

With each passing day, Friday's English improved. Soon we were able to talk about a great many things. One day, Friday told me that he had been to my island before. He showed me the place where he and his people had landed. It was on the other side of the island, where I had found the footprint! He said that they had eaten prisoners taken in war.

So Friday was a cannibal, too!

I had been afraid of this, but I had hoped

and prayed that it wasn't true. Now I made Friday promise me that he would never again eat human flesh. As long as I knew him, this was a promise that he kept.

For the next three years, Friday and I lived alone on the island. The cannibals did not return, and we were very happy.

9 The Mutiny

One morning I was fast asleep when Friday came running into my room. "Master, Master, they are come, they are come!" he said. He was pointing out to the sea.

I jumped out of bed, got dressed, and grabbed my telescope. With Friday close behind me, I ran to the top of the hill behind the fortress. Sure enough, I could see the sails of a ship not far from shore. It looked like an English vessel! Peering through the telescope, I also saw a longboat heading toward the beach.

The sight of the ship and the longboat filled my heart with joy. I could hardly believe my own eyes! Men from my own country would soon set foot on my island! But as I watched them, the feeling of joy faded. Something didn't seem quite right. I asked myself what an English ship was doing in this part of the world. For 28 years I had not seen another English ship. Perhaps these men were up to no good. I decided it wouldn't be safe to run down and greet them right away. I did not want to fall into the hands of pirates or killers.

When the longboat reached the shore, its passengers stepped onto the beach. I counted ten men. Two of them carried guns and several carried swords. It looked to me as if three of the men were being taken ashore as prisoners. Their hands were tied. One of the prisoners seemed to be asking or begging for something. A sailor raised a sword as if to strike the man.

I had no idea what was going on. Friday called out to me in English as best he could, "O Master! You see English mans eat prisoner as well as savage mans."

"Friday," I said, "do you think they are going to *eat* them? No, no! I am afraid they will kill those men. But you may be sure that Englishmen will not *eat* anyone!"

The sailors left their prisoners alone and walked off toward the woods. The three prisoners sat down on the beach, although they could have walked away, too. But it looked as if they didn't know what to do.

"Friday," I said, "we must find out who those men are and what is going on. It looks like they could use our help." We went back to the fortress and got our guns and knives. Then we went down to the beach and walked up to the prisoners. When they saw us, they looked as if they wanted to run away. We must have been a strange sight, indeed.

"Gentlemen," I said. "Do not be afraid of me. You may have a friend on this lonely island you did not expect!"

"You must have been sent from heaven, sir!" cried one of the men. "Are you a real man, or an angel?"

"*All* our help is from heaven," I said. "But I am a man—an Englishman. I am willing to help you. My servant and I have guns. So how can we help you? What is your story?"

"Our story is too long to tell, while those killers are so near," said the man. "In short, I was captain of that ship. My men had mutinied against me. They wanted to kill me, but I was able to talk them out of it. At last they set me ashore on this island, with these two men. One is my mate, the other a passenger. They expect us to *die* here!"

I told the captain that I would be glad to help him get back his ship. But in return I asked him to promise that he would take

Friday and me back to England.

"You have my word," said the captain. For the first time there was a faint look of hope shining in his eyes. "Once the ship is mine again, you shall indeed sail with us to England. And I will let the whole world know that I owe you my life!"

I gave guns to the captain and his men.

They went off looking for the sailors. When they caught up with them, there was a brief battle. The captain killed two of the sailors, and the other five were taken prisoner. Friday and the captain's men then locked the prisoners in our goat pen.

I invited the captain to dine with me in the fortress. I told him about my many years of living on the island. He was amazed by my story. I think he found it hard to believe. But when he saw all the things I had built— the fortress, the cave, the walls and fences— he knew I was telling the truth.

Late in the day, another longboat came ashore with 10 more sailors from the ship. The sailors spread out searching for their missing mates. After dark, they returned to the longboat a few at a time. We were ready for them. The captain killed their leader, and we tied up the others.

The captain told the men that sailors who mutiny at sea are hanged for their crime. Many of the sailors said they had been forced by others to act against the captain. They begged to be given a chance to help the captain get his ship back.

Later that night the captain took the two longboats and some men. I wished him good luck. Somehow I was quite sure that he'd be able to take back his ship. I slept soundly that night. The next morning I was awakened by joyful shouts. "The ship is yours! The ship is yours!" It was the captain. He was smiling as he came up to my fortress. "My friend," he said, clasping my hand, "the ship is all yours, and so are we."

The captain gave me a suit of his clothes. "Try this on," he said. I hadn't worn clothes such as these in more than 20 years. It felt very strange. By now I was used to clothes made from animal skins. "Think about what things you want to bring with you on the ship," the captain said.

Before we could sail, we had to decide what to do with the five prisoners in the goat pen. The captain said that these men were dangerous. He could not trust them. He did not want them on his ship, even in chains. I told the captain we could leave the men on the island. I could show them what they would need to know in order to survive.

We walked to the goat pen to talk to the prisoners. They looked worried when they saw us. Maybe they thought we planned to kill them. "We are giving you a choice," I said. "If you sail back to England with us, you will hang for your crime. If you stay here on the island, you will have to work hard. But you can live a good life here."

The men chose to remain on the island. They knew they were lucky to be given such a choice. I gave them my fortress and my country home. I showed them how to grow grain, bake bread, plant corn, harvest grapes, and raise goats for milk and cheese.

Then I gathered the few things I wanted to bring with me on the ship. I took my umbrella, my goatskin cap, and Poll, my parrot. I also remembered to take the money I had saved from the shipwreck so many years ago. At last, Friday and I went aboard the ship. It was December 19, 1686. After 28 years, 2 months, and 19 days, I was finally leaving the island.

Back to England

After a long sea voyage, Friday and I arrived in England on June 11, 1687. We went first to the city of York, where I learned that my mother and father had died. I found my two sisters, who were very happy to see me. Both were poor and lived out in the country. It made me sad to see that life had not been kinder to them. One of my sisters was a widow. The other had a husband who did not treat her very well. I also learned that the two sons of the brother I never knew were living in York.

I felt like a total stranger in England. It was as if I had never been known there. I didn't quite know what to do with my life. The little money that I had would not last very long. I began to wonder what had become of my sugar plantation in Brazil. To find out, I would have to travel to Lisbon in Portugal. Unfortunately, I didn't have enough money to make the trip.

While I was trying to figure out what to do, I met with a fine piece of gratitude which I didn't expect. The captain whose life I had saved from the mutineers sent for me. He invited me to meet the owners of his ship. To thank me for saving their vessel, they gave me 200 pounds as my reward. This was more than enough money to pay for the trip to Lisbon!

I soon booked passage on a ship bound for Lisbon. There, with any luck, I could get news of my plantation. Friday came with me. As on all occasions, he proved to be a wonderful traveling companion.

In Lisbon I found my old friend, the sea captain who had saved me when I escaped from North Africa. He had good news for me. The man in Brazil who had managed my plantation all these years had done a good job. I was now a wealthy man!

I was ready to return to England. But because I had been so unfortunate at sea, I decided to travel over land. I couldn't rid myself of a strange feeling that we might get caught in a storm at sea. So I bought two horses, guns, and other supplies. We joined a small group of merchants who would also be traveling that way. Soon Friday and I were riding north.

Our route back to England took us over the Pyrenees Mountains, near the borders of Spain and France. It was the middle of winter. As we got closer to the mountains, a cold wind began to blow. Poor Friday was really frightened when he saw the whitecapped mountains. He had never seen snow or felt the sting of cold weather!

In the town of Pampeluna we hired a guide to lead our group over the mountains. This part of our trip proved to be difficult indeed. As we climbed higher and higher, we were caught in a terrible snowstorm. At times, we could hardly see where we were going. I feared for the perishing of our fingers and toes! We were lucky we didn't freeze to death.

We were also lucky that we had guns. As we slowly made our way through the snowstorm, we were attacked by hungry wolves. We shot several of them, and the rest ran away. Finally we reached the other side of the mountains. I said to Friday, "I shall never cross those mountains again. I would rather meet with a storm at sea!"

When we arrived in England, I found somebody who wanted to buy my plantation. I sold it to him for 33,000 pieces of gold. Now I was a *very* rich man, indeed!

I went to York, where I settled down and got married. I gave some money to my two sisters. I also found my two nephews and took them into my care. I raised the older one as a gentleman. The other boy was drawn to the sea. I sent him to sea for five years. He proved himself to be a brave lad, so I later made him captain of his own ship.

In 1694 my wife died. It was then that I found myself thinking once more of my

island. My nephew was about to sail to that part of the world on a trading trip. He invited me to come along. So Friday and I went to sea again. Later that year we arrived at the island where I had lived for so long.

There we were greeted by the five sailors we had left behind. They seemed in good spirits and were glad to see us. They told us that they had been happy on the island and that living there had made them better men. Then they showed us the work they had done. They had not only taken care of my farm, but built several other farms as well.

I left them a supply of many necessary things. Then I divided my island into parts and gave each sailor a part as his own. I kept much of it for myself, thinking that someday I might wish to return.

And so, my life of adventure, which had begun so foolishly, ended happily.